SPINOSAURUS
(SPINE-oh-SORE-us)

TYRANNOSAURUS REX
(tie-RAN-oh-sore-us rex)

APATOSAURUS
(ah-PAT-oh-sore-us)

VELOCIRAPTOR
(vel-OSS-ee-rap-tor)

To Rose and Harry, with love
T.K.

For Elin, the master of hide and seeks
S.W.

First published in 2015 by Scholastic Children's Books
Euston House, 24 Eversholt Street
London NW1 1DB
a division of Scholastic Ltd
www.scholastic.co.uk
London ~ New York ~ Toronto ~ Sydney ~ Auckland
Mexico City ~ New Delhi ~ Hong Kong

Text copyright © 2015 Timothy Knapman
Illustrations copyright © 2015 Sarah Warburton
PB ISBN 978 1 4071 4586 0
All rights reserved
Printed in Malaysia

1 3 5 7 9 10 8 6 4 2

The moral rights of Timothy Knapman and Sarah Warburton have been assert

Papers used by Scholastic Children's Books are made from wood grown in sustaina

Dinosaurs in my School

TRICERATOPS
(tri-SERRA-tops)

STEGOSAURUS
(STEG-oh-SORE-us)

PTEROSAUR
(TERR-oh-sore)

HADROSAURUS
(HAD-row-SORE-us)

ANKYLOSAURUS
(an-KIE-loh-sore-us)

PARASAUROLOPHUS
(pa-ra-saw-ROL-off-us)

IGUANODON
(ig-WHA-noh-don)

Dinosaurs
in my
School

By Timothy Knapman

Illustrated by Sarah Warburton

SCHOLASTIC

There aren't any dinosaurs in my street —
I know, I'm not a fool.
You don't see a T. rex in the park
Or Iguanodons at the pool.
So tell me, please, oh why oh why...

Are there **dinosaurs** in my **school?**

SCHOOL

There's an Ankylosaur in the Art Room!
He's spraying paint around...

While the Hadrosaurs play silly games
With all the glitter they've found!

I try to make a picture,
But the moment that it's done...

Apatosaurus eats it
And my crayons, just for fun!

"There are dinosaurs in my school!" I say,
But the teachers just don't see.
When they find that dreadful mess
They're sure to think it's me.

I'll go and play
some music...

No!

Stegosaurus got there first.
He broke the drums and tambourines
And his singing is the worst!

"There are DINOSAURS in our school!" I yell.
"We have to get them out!"
But Miss Brown says, "Sit still and shush.
It's not polite to shout."

There's no escape when it's time to eat.

A Pterosaur's pinched my food!
And when I say, "Hey, put that back!"
He makes a noise that's rude.

After lunch, we go outside
To run and jump and play,
But with all these naughty dinosaurs
There'll be no games today.

Triceratops pops footballs...

Velociraptor wins the race...

Spinosaurus steals the goal posts,
But the teachers won't give chase!

"Oh goodness me... Look!

DINOSAURS!

That boy was right!" they yelp,
And when they run away, I say,
"Will **somebody** please help?"

Our school is full of every kind
Of prehistoric creature!
But I know who will put things right
And that's our brave Head Teacher.

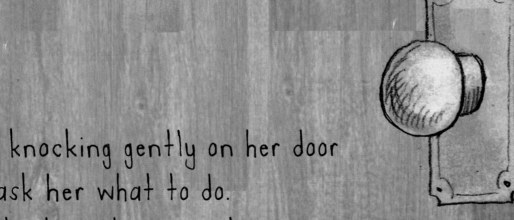

So knocking gently on her door
I ask her what to do.
But when she comes to answer me...

She's a **dinosaur** too!

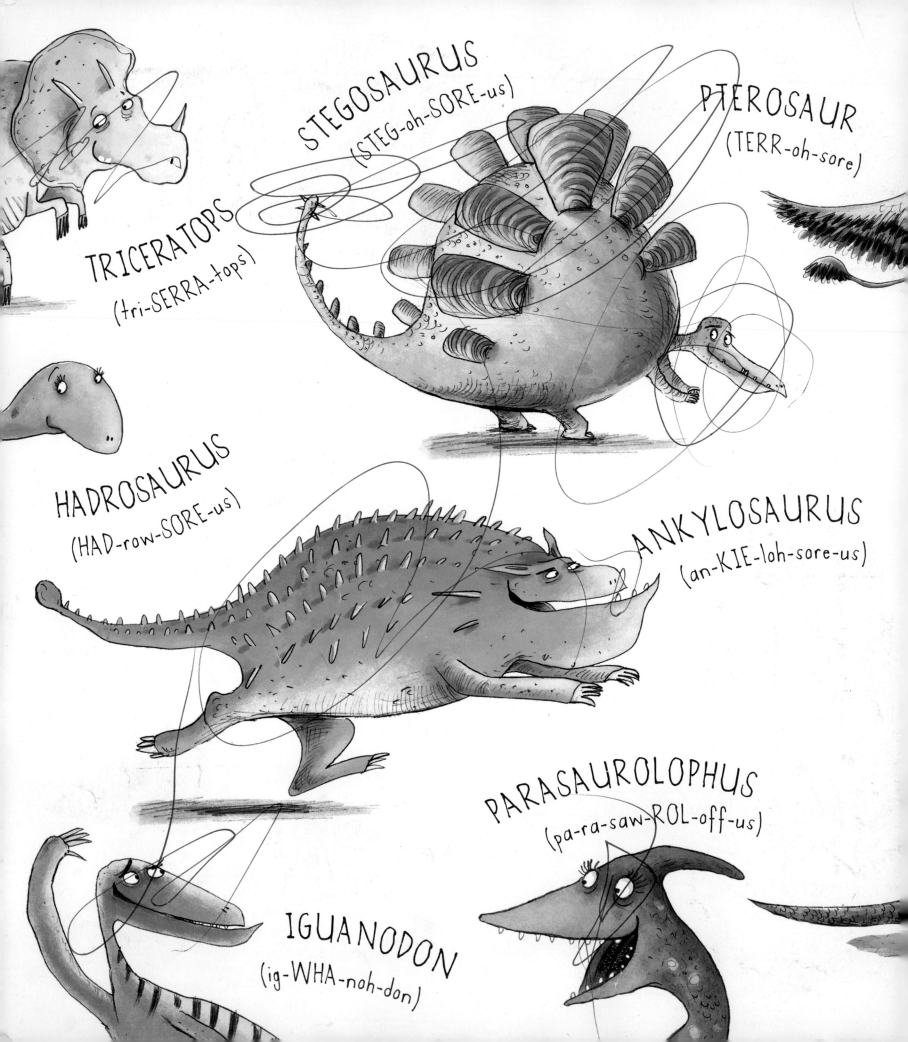

TRICERATOPS
(tri-SERRA-tops)

STEGOSAURUS
(STEG-oh-SORE-us)

PTEROSAUR
(TERR-oh-sore)

HADROSAURUS
(HAD-row-SORE-us)

ANKYLOSAURUS
(an-KIE-loh-sore-us)

PARASAUROLOPHUS
(pa-ra-saw-ROL-off-us)

IGUANODON
(ig-WHA-noh-don)

SPINOSAURUS
(SPINE-oh-SORE-us)

TYRANNOSAURUS REX
(tie-RAN-oh-sore-us rex)

APATOSAURUS
(ah-PAT-oh-sore-us)

VELOCIRAPTOR
(vel-OSS-ee-rap-tor)

Splat!